If you could ~~SCHOOL LIBRARY~~
what would ~~~~

Jot them down here!

MY WISH LIST*

1 _____
_____

2 _____
_____

3 _____
_____

*YOU <u>CAN'T</u> WISH FOR MORE WISHES,
SO DON'T EVEN BOTHER TRYING!

Books by Steven Lenton

The Genie and Teeny books in reading order:

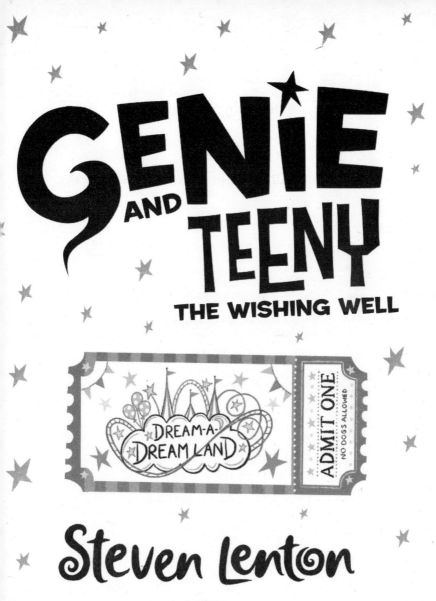

GENIE AND TEENY

THE WISHING WELL

ADMIT ONE

NO DOGS ALLOWED

DREAM-A-DREAM LAND

Steven Lenton

HarperCollins *Children's Books*

First published in the United Kingdom by
HarperCollins *Children's Books* in 2022
HarperCollins *Children's Books* is a division of HarperCollins*Publishers* Ltd
1 London Bridge Street
London SE1 9GF

www.harpercollins.co.uk

HarperCollins*Publishers*
1st Floor, Watermarque Building, Ringsend Road
Dublin 4, Ireland

1

ISBN 978–0–00–840855–8

MIX
Paper from
responsible sources

FSC™ C007454

This book is produced from independently certified FSC™ paper
to ensure responsible forest management.

For more information visit: www.harpercollins.co.uk/green

FOR THE cheeky CHILDREN at
ALVESTON PRIMARY SCHOOL! SL x

HELLO, READER!

When we last left Genie and Teeny, they were having a well-earned nap inside Grant's 'NOT-A-TEAPOT' teapot (let's call it a tea-lamp from now on!) with Teeny's owner, Tilly, after a **VERY** long day at Tilly's school.

But do you remember what happened next? That's right, Tilly's mum walked into Tilly's bedroom and heard all MANNER of sounds coming from the tea-lamp!

And this is exactly where we join them all now . . .

CHAPTER 1
WAKE UP, QUICK!

Grant was in a deep sleep, *snoring* and having a lovely dream about being back home in Genie World with his family.

Tilly was smiling in her sleep, having a dream about her three wishes.

Teeny was dribbling in his
sleep, having a dream
about giant sausages.

'Tilly, TILLY,
where are you?' her mum
called, picking up the tea-lamp.

Teeny woke up from his dream – oh, and
he'd just got to a really good bit! Frantically,
he licked Tilly's cheek as he tried desperately

to wake her up. What would happen if Mum

discovered them in the tea-lamp with a genie?

'Hee hee, Teeny, get off!' Tilly giggled herself awake. Teeny looked at Tilly, tilted his head to one side, lifted one of his ears and pointed up with one of his paws, signalling her to listen.

'Tilly – where **are** you and what's going on with this teapot?' Mum's voice boomed.

'**oh no!** We fell asleep!' Tilly whispered, and she started to shake Grant. 'Grant, **WAKE UP**, quick!' she said, pouring a glass of sparkly water over his face.

'Wha-**what's** going on? I was having a lovely dream about my dad and sister. They were wearing silly hats. **Gosh,** I miss them SO much,' Grant replied sadly.

'Grant,' Tilly whispered, 'Mum is in my room, and we are in the tea-lamp, way smaller than normal, and about to be in SERIOUS trouble if she finds us in this state!'

'Don't worry, Tilly. I have a plan,' Grant replied confidently.

'Oh dear,' said Tilly, looking worriedly at Teeny, who also looked rather concerned.

Mum picked up the tea-lamp and was just about to lift the lid when . . .

Grant sat up, twiddled his nose and snapped his fingers.

DING-

DONG!

The front doorbell rang JUST in the nick of time.

Mum put the teapot back on the bed and went downstairs to see who was at the door.

'QUICK, Grant! You need to get me and Teeny back to normal size before Mum comes back!' Tilly said.

'No problem!' Grant nodded, as he said his magic wishy word:

'Alaka-blam-a-bumwhistle!'

Tilly shot up into the air, her head sticking out of the top of the teapot and one arm poking out of the spout.

'Grant, this isn't quite what I had in mind!'
she cried. 'Try again quickly!'

'Whoops, sorry, Tilly!' Grant
clicked his fingers and – POW! – in a cloud
of turquoise smoke and sparkly stars, Tilly
and Teeny were normal size again . . .

Except that Tilly had Teeny's body, and Teeny had Tilly's body!

'woof, woof, woof, woof, WOOF!' woofed Tilly . . . or was it Teeny? It was tricky to tell.

'Oh no!' shouted Grant! 'Not again! Third time lucky, I hope—!'

I think we need your help, reader! Can you concentrate and twiddle your nose as you turn the page?

YES! Well done, reader. It worked!
'**WOOF!**' said Tilly.

'Oh no, it DIDN'T work!' cried Grant.

'ʜᴇᴇ ʜᴇᴇ,' Tilly giggled. 'Only kidding! It DID work. Well done, Grant!'

'**WOOF!**' woofed Teeny.

At that moment, they heard the sound of Mum's footsteps coming back up the stairs. Then, suddenly, she burst into the room.

'**Tilly!** Where— Oh, **THERE** you are! Where were you when I was calling you earlier?' Mum asked, folding her arms.

'Sorry, Mum, we were brushing our teeth, **weren't we,** Teeny?' she fibbed.

Teeny smiled a big smile at Mum.

'**Hmm**, okay,' said Mum, 'but there's something going on with that teapot. There were some very funny noises coming from inside.' Mum looked at it, puzzled.

But Tilly looked down at the tea-lamp with a little smile. Grant was peeping out through the crack in the teapot and blushed.

'**Right**, breakfast time, you two!' Mum shouted as she headed back down the stairs.

Tilly picked up the tea-lamp and Grant popped his head out of the top.

'**Phew!** That was close!' Tilly said. 'After breakfast, let's make a plan about how to get you back to Genie World. Okay, Grant?'

'**Excellent** idea, Tilly! I can't wait to see my family again,' Grant replied, hiding back inside the pot.

CHAPTER 2
BREAKFAST PLANS

'**Right**, here's your breakfast,' Mum said in a rush, putting down two bowls, one on the table with dog food in it, and one on the floor containing porridge. Tilly and Teeny both looked at their bowls and **screwed** up their faces. Tilly swapped the bowls around and they both wolfed down their food.

'Right, my darlings,' said Mum. 'I'm off to the study to get some work done. You wouldn't believe how many phone calls I have to make and emails I have to send today! Give me a shout if you need me – and try not to get into any trouble!' she called, closing the study door behind her.

'Wow,' said Grant. 'Your mum's a busy lady, Tilly! It's so nice that you're here with her, even if she is on the phone a lot of the time. She clearly loves you very much.'

Grant clicked his fingers and the photograph of his dad and sister appeared in his hands.

'I'm really, **really** missing my dad and sister today. I wonder what they're up to,' Grant said as a tear rolled down his cheek and dropped on to the picture of his family.

Teeny put his paw on Grant's hand to reassure him, then he looked up at Tilly.

'Well, now the coast is clear, Grant, let's hatch a plan,' Tilly said.

'Hatch a plan? Like hatching an egg? I'm a **GENIE** not a **CHICKEN,** Tilly!'

'It's a turn of phrase, Grant,' Tilly replied. 'It means, let's make a plan for how to get you back to Genie World so you can see your dad and sister again! But first we need to know where Genie World is.'

'Well, Genie World, or (to give it its official title) WISHALUZIA, is **miles** and **MILES** away,' Grant explained.

'Like miles away across the **SEA** somewhere?' Tilly asked.

'No, no! Like high, high, high

up in the **SKY.** The queen's guards threw me and my lamp off the farthest corner of WISHALUZIA and I tumbled down for **THOUSANDS** of miles, shooting past stars and whizzing through clouds, until finally I crashed here on Earth.'

Hmm, thought

Tilly, rubbing her chin with wonder. 'So we need to come up with a way to get you as high up into the sky as possible . . . Oh, I think I have an idea! Perhaps I can wish you back to WISHALUZIA?'

'I'm afraid you can't, and neither can I,' Grant replied. 'I can't just magic myself back to Genie World, because Queen Mizelda cast a magical spell to keep me out! It makes my tummy feel funny when I think about how much I miss my family and how I might never see them again.'

'Grant, when I'm away from home, I sometimes feel funny too,' Tilly said. 'Mum calls it being **homesick**. I think that must be how you are feeling today.' Tilly gave him a hug. 'I know something that might cheer you up. Where's your joke book?'

Grant disappeared into the tea-lamp and reappeared with his big joke book. He handed it to Tilly, who flicked through the pages until she found a really, **really** funny joke.

'Okay, Grant.

What has a T at the beginning, a T in the middle and a T at the end?'

Grant thought hard. 'Er, I dunno.' He scratched his head.

'**A TEAPOT!**'

Tilly cried and she giggled.

Grant sort of chuckled but he still looked very sad.

'Ooh, what about this one,' Tilly said, trying again.

'**Why did the genie hate genie school? . . . Because all they did was**

SPELLING!'

Grant attempted a smile, but he had to admit it – he was still feeling pretty glum.

Tilly tried again. 'This one will DEFINITELY cheer you up.

Did you know that every genie has a fish?...Yes, they all have a

MAGIC CARP-PET!'

But Grant just looked really sad now and his tummy started to rumble.

'Oh dear – you really are homesick, aren't you?' Tilly said. 'What we need is some kind

of vehicle to get us high into the sky, like . . .
an **aeroplane** or a **rocket,** so we can
get you back home!'

Tilly started to feel hopeful. She ran upstairs
to her room, grabbed her crafting box and
hurried back down to the kitchen.

Grant looked at the box. 'Now, I love
crafting as much as anyone, Tilly,' he said.
'But even I can't make a rocket out of a
cardboard box!'

Tilly giggled. 'Oh, Grant, you are **funny!**
No, it's to make a plan, silly!'

She took out a large, rolled-up piece of
paper, and spread it out on the kitchen table.

Then she grabbed her materials and started sketching. Art and Design was Tilly's favourite subject at school – and you could tell. She did a REALLY good drawing. Grant and Teeny looked on in amazement as Tilly swirled and scribbled using her crayons, pencils and paints.

'TA-DAH!' Tilly shouted, holding up her drawing.

'Presenting the Elastic Fantastic Flying **MACHINE!**'

'OoooOOOOooooooh!' exclaimed Grant, looking more closely at the plan. 'Let's go into the garden and try to make it!'

CHAPTER 3

GOODBYE, GRANT!

Tilly, Teeny and Grant headed to the garden

shed and took out everything they needed.

They used a garden swing as a frame. Then

they tied a tyre and two old hammocks to it.

Then they crafted a rocket-shaped vehicle out

of Tilly's old toy car and a cardboard box.

'OOOoh, I have the perfect hat for such an

occasion!' Grant exclaimed. He flew into his

tea-lamp and reappeared

wearing a fancy cape

and a very snazzy

crash helmet with

goggles. 'Thank

you both **so much**

for helping me to get back

home,' Grant said. 'I know I only met you

a short while ago, but I feel like I've been

friends with you all my life. We've had such

fun times together,' he added with a tear

in his eye.

'We're really going to miss you, Grant,' replied Tilly, trying not to cry as she and Teeny gave Grant the biggest **hug** in the world.

Grant got into the rocket, placed the goggles over his eyes and Tilly and Teeny pulled it back with all their might.

Grant shouted out a countdown:

'Three,

two,

ONE –

LAUNCH!!!'

Tilly and Teeny let go and Grant hurtled through the air.

'WOOOoHOOOOOOOOOOOOO!

he cried as he waved back at Tilly and Teeny.
He **sailed** past bees, butterflies, birds, and . . .

. . . DONK! –

he went

STRAIGHT
into a
tall tree!

Grant tumbled
out of the
cardboard
rocket and
started to fall.

'GAAAAAA-
AAAAAH!'

he screamed as
he hurtled
back down
to the ground.

Quickly, he pressed a button on the side of
his crash helmet and helicopter blades and two
joystick controllers folded out of the machine.

Carefully, he steered himself back to Tilly's
garden.

'TILLY! TEENY!' he shouted
excitedly.

'I'M BAAAAACK!'

And before Tilly and Teeny had time to turn around, Grant had crash-landed on top of them with a **BANG** and they fell in a heap on the ground.

'Grant! **WHAT happened?**' asked Tilly.

'Somebody put a tree in the way!' Grant replied, shaking leaves out of his ears. 'But I don't think I would have got high enough to reach WISHALUZIA, even if the tree hadn't been there. **Thanks** for trying, though, Tilly.' Grant looked sad but was still smiling.

'Well, we can't give up,' said Tilly. 'It's back to the drawing board, I guess.' And they all giggled.

CHAPTER 4

PLAN B

'I think we need a break and some brain food,' said Grant. 'What do you fancy, Tilly?'

'OOOh, I fancy some chips and a Coke float, please!' Tilly said.

'Coming **right up!**' Grant replied.

Grant wiggled his nose and said his magic wishy word:

'Alaka-blam-a-bumWhistle!'

'Oh, Grant!' laughed Tilly.

Grant opened his eyes to see . . .

. . . Tilly and Teeny surrounded by some ships and a joke goat!

'**Sorry!**' shouted Grant. He clapped his hands and the ships and joke goat turned into chips and a Coke float.

'Thank you, Grant,' said Tilly as she gave Teeny one of her chips.

The trio went into the living room to discuss a new plan. Suddenly a loud advert blurted out from the television.

'COME TO

DREAM-A-DREAM LAND –

the BIGGEST, WILDEST, *FUNNIEST* theme park EVER!

And now home to the TALLEST ride in the world, the

CRAZY CLOUD COASTER

– so crazy-HIGH it flies MILES into the SKY!

Nowwwwww OPEN!'

'WOW, Grant! Did you hear that? A roller coaster that flies up INTO THE CLOUDS!' Tilly exclaimed excitedly.

'Yes, it sounds amazing,' Grant replied. 'But I really think we should be focusing on how I can get back up to . . . AAAHHH, TILLY!' he cried, suddenly realising. 'WE COULD GO ON THE CRAZY CLOUD COASTER!'

Tilly and Teeny looked at each other and rolled their eyes.

'EXACTLY, Grant! We could go on the ride, and when it is at its highest point in the sky, you could cloud-hop to WISHALUZIA! Then you could work out how to get inside and back to your family!'

'**WOOF!**' woofed Teeny in agreement, wagging his tail.

'The only problem is, DREAM-A-DREAM LAND is **MILES** away. It will probably be closed by the time we get there.' Tilly sighed. 'I wish we were there right now!'

Tilly clasped her hands over her mouth as she realised that she had accidentally made her very first wish! But before she had a moment to blink, Grant had twiddled his nose and said his magic wishy word:

'Alaka-blam-a-bumwhistle!'

There standing next to them was a white
cow, looking very confused.

Tilly laughed. 'I said RIGHT NOW not
WHITE COW!'

'I'll try again!' said Grant, closing his eyes
and really concentrating this time.

'Alaka-blam-a-bumwhistle!'

he shouted, then he slowly opened his eyes

and saw . . .

They were standing outside

DREAM-A-DREAM LAND!

CHAPTER 5

'WOW, Grant! **YOU DID IT!**' Tilly

said. 'And it only took you two tries. That's

wonderful!' Tilly beamed.

A clown was shouting outside a kiosk by the theme park gates. 'TICKETS! GET YOUR TICKETS!'

Tilly was about to buy a ticket with the emergency money her mum had given her (well, this was kind of an emergency – Grant needed to get home to his family!) when a very angry-looking security guard shouted, '**NO DOGS ALLOWED!**' and then pointed to a sign.

'Oh, sorry,' said Tilly. 'I didn't realise, sir.' Tilly picked Teeny up in her arms and walked away from the gates. 'Grant, what are we going to do?' she turned to her friend. 'We can't leave Teeny on his own out here. That means we

can't even go into the park, let alone get on the **CRAZY CLOUD COASTER!**

Grant had a look around and saw lots of families walking into the park. There were boys, girls, grandmas, grandads, mums, dads . . . and all manner of families.

'I have an idea, Tilly!' he said. 'Why don't I turn Teeny into a human boy? Then he will be allowed into the park and he can come on all the rides with us!'

'That's a **great** idea! It's definitely worth a try,' said Tilly with a grin.

Teeny **gulped.**

Grant closed his eyes, wiggled his nose and said:

'Alaka-blam-a-bumWhistle!'

'Grant! We said a **BOY**, not a TOY!'
said Tilly.

Grant tried again, but this time Teeny
turned into a saveloy, which Teeny found
very frustrating because his favourite food was
sausages – so being one was very strange!

'Uh-oh, third time lucky!' said Grant,
wiggling his fingers and uttering another

'Alaka-blam-a-bumWhistle!'

Did it work this time?

Well, sort of . . .

Grant had turned MOST of Teeny into a boy, but boy-Teeny still had his fluffy ears and his tail!

'Well, I think we can work with this, Grant,' said Tilly. 'We can hide his ears under a hat and tuck his tail into his shorts.'

Grant popped back into his tea-lamp and came out again with a big hat. He put the hat on Teeny's head and tied it under his chin. Then Teeny tucked his tail into his shorts.

'Oooh, I wonder if he can talk human,' Grant asked excitedly, looking at Teeny.

'WOOF!' woofed Teeny.

'Oh. I guess that answers that, then,' Grant sighed.

'WOOF!' Teeny woofed again.

'Please try not to woof, Teeny,' Tilly said. 'It will give you away.'

'**WOO—**' Teeny nearly said, putting his hand over his mouth.

'Now you just need a human name and we can go into the park!' said Tilly, thinking. 'What about . . . **Timmy?**'

Teeny shook his head.

'**Terence?**'

Teeny shook his head again.

'**Tallulah?**' Grant offered.

Teeny stuck his tongue out and blew a raspberry.

Then Teeny looked excited and pointed at a sign outside the park.

'Teeny, no! We can't call you Toilet!' Tilly told him.

Teeny folded his arms in a huff.

'Let's just stick to calling you Teeny. Now, come on – we haven't got a moment to lose!'

CHAPTER 6
INTO THE PARK

Tilly, Teeny and Grant returned to the kiosk at the entrance of the park, bought two tickets, took a map and walked up to the gates.

The security guard instantly recognised Tilly

and called over to her, 'Oi, what happened to your dog?'

'Oh, er, my mum just picked him up and took him home,' Tilly replied.

'That was quick, and who's this?' he said, pointing at boy-Teeny.

'This? Oh, this is my ... er ... my brother! He was running late!'

Tilly read the name on the security guard's badge: **Sidney Snoop.**

Sidney Snoop rubbed his chin. 'Hmm, okay. In you go,' he said, looking unsure. 'But

no funny business. I'm keeping my eye on you two.'

Tilly and Teeny walked on through the gates and into the park, but just before they disappeared into the crowd, Teeny's tail BOINGED out of his shorts and started to wag!

Sidney Snoop noticed.

'What on **earth** . . . ?' he muttered to himself and started to follow them . . .

CHAPTER 7

FINDING THE
CRAZY CLOUD COASTER!

Tilly unfolded the map of the park.

'Right. We are down HERE and the CRAZY CLOUD COASTER is up HERE,' she said, marking the two points on the map with a red pen she had in her rucksack.

Grant floated down to the map and grabbed the pen. 'Oooh, and look!' he said. 'There are lots of food stands . . . oooh, and souvenir shops . . . and look at all the other rides too!'

'Grant,' said Tilly, 'you're getting distracted. We just need to find the **CRAZY CLOUD COASTER** and get you home, isn't that right, Teeny . . . Teeny? Teeny – where are you?' Tilly started to panic.

Suddenly they heard someone shouting:

'OI, YOU!'

Tilly and Grant looked up to see Sidney Snoop running towards a queue of people who were all waiting to get on to the **SAUSAGE FALLS FLUME** ride.

Tilly gasped. 'Grant, there's **Teeny** at the front of the queue! He must think the giant sausage boats are real! **Quick,** we need to get to him before Sidney the security guard does!' she cried.

Tilly and Grant raced towards Teeny, but Sidney Snoop was already nearly at the front of the queue.

'STOP THAT BOY!' Sidney yelled.

'TEENY!' Tilly shouted, racing off towards the front of the queue.

But they were too late. Teeny had hopped into one of the sausage-shaped boats, started licking it and floated off, unaware that he was causing such a kerfuffle behind him.

'STOP THAT SAUSAGE!' shouted Sidney, and he jumped into the next boat. Tilly and Grant jumped into the boat after that.

Teeny turned around to see what was going on and saw Sidney crawling along his sausage boat towards him. Teeny yelped

TURN BACK!

BEWARE!!!

and scampered to the front of his sausage boat. Sidney stood up and tried to jump into Teeny's boat, but it was very wobbly and he fell backwards with a bump.

Then the boats went through some dark tunnels and around some sharp turns, and

STAY IN YOUR SAUSAGE!

suddenly came to an abrupt **HALT**. The
sausage boats slowly started to climb the
tallest section of the ride . . .

DON'T
BANGER
YOUR HEAD!

Teeny looked back nervously as Sidney
was clambering up and out of *his* again. He
looked like he was actually going to jump

on to Teeny's boat this time. As they climbed

higher and higher towards the top of the ride,

Sidney stood proudly on top of his sausage.

NOW I'VE GOT YOU, BOY-DOG!' he shouted at Teeny. 'I KNOW YOU'RE A DOG IN DISGUISE! And dogs are **NOT ALLOWED HERE!**' he hollered.

'He's not a dog – he's my BROTHER!' Tilly called out from behind him. 'Grant, we need to **DO** something!'

But Grant didn't need to do anything, because just as Sidney Snoop jumped up, Sidney's collar caught on the giant mechanical fork that was moving up and down at the top of the track.

'GAAAAAAH!!'

Sidney shouted.

'**WOO-HOOOooOOOoooOF!**'

Teeny woofed in delight as his
sausage boat **ZOOMED**
down the flume at break-neck
speed, his tongue and ears flapping
in the breeze.

Sidney's empty boat was

followed by Tilly and Grant who both chuckled as they **WHOOSHED** underneath Sidney, who was still stuck on the giant fork.

'I'LL GET YOU AND YOUR FUNNY DOG TOO!' Sidney shouted as they sped off down the flume.

At the bottom of the ride, Teeny was waiting for Tilly and Grant.

'Teeny, don't wander off again! You could have really got us into trouble back there,' Tilly warned him. 'Grant, we need another hat to cover his ears!'

'No problem!' replied Grant. He flew down the spout of his tea-lamp and reappeared with an even bigger hat, popped it on Teeny's head and this time double-knotted the flaps under his chin.

CHAPTER 8

A SNOOPY SQUELCH!

'**Right**,' Tilly said. 'Back to business, you two. We need to find the **CRAZY CLOUD COASTER.** Now, where did I put the park map?' She took off her rucksack and rummaged inside, placing Grant's tea-lamp on the side of a stall

81

so she could get right to the bottom of the bag.

'Ah, here it is! Right, so now we are HERE, and we need to get HERE.' Tilly drew on the map again as she spoke. 'It looks like the quickest way is via the gift shop, through the funhouse and around the MAGIC FLYING CARPET ride, then we will finally be at the CRAZY CLOUD COASTER!'

Suddenly, they heard a faint squelching sound. Tilly looked up to see a VERY angry, very wet, very tired-looking Sidney Snoop in the distance. He was soaked to the skin, his shoes full of water. Sidney spotted them and shouted: **'STOP!'**

ARCADE

SAUSAGE FALLS

GIFT SHOP

'Quick, we have to **hurry!**' Tilly whispered.

Tilly, Genie and Teeny ran off towards the gift shop, not realising that they had left the tea-lamp behind.

Sidney Snoop squelched after them but stopped to pick up the tea-lamp.

'Why on earth are they carrying a cracked old teapot around?' he said to himself. 'They must have stolen it from the gift shop. I'll keep hold of this! Ooh, I think I need a sit-down first, though. My poor back is killing me.' And he sat down in a very fancy-looking seat.

Suddenly there was a strange clunking and whirring sound and Sidney Snoop started spinning round and round! He hadn't realised that he was in one of the teacups in the SUPER-SPINNY SICKLY SAUCERS ride – and it was spinning faster and faster and FASTER.

Sidney clung on to the teapot for dear life as he started to scream. He turned green and felt very, very ill.

CHAPTER 9

WHERE iS THE TEA-LAMP?

Tilly, Grant and Teeny ran into the gift shop,

past rows and rows of sweets, T-shirts, toys

and teapots with the theme park logo on.

Seeing the park teapots made Tilly stop

dead in her tracks. 'Grant, where's your

tea-lamp?' she asked, turning pale.

'It's in your rucksack, isn't it?' he replied.

Tilly looked inside her bag and, just as she thought, the tea-lamp was nowhere to be found. She gulped. 'It's **not** in here! We **left it behind** the teacup ride! **Quick,** we need to run back and get it!'

'Don't worry, Tilly. I'll **whizz** back for it,' Grant offered. But before he had the chance to do anything, he had **disappeared** in a cloud of turquoise smoke!

'Grant! Where have you gone?' Tilly cried.

CHAPTER 10

SiDNEY SNOOP'S WiSH

Well, you see, readers, what had happened was this . . .

While Sidney Snoop was spinning round and round in the teacup, hugging Grant's tea-lamp and trying not to be sick, the bristles of his moustache rubbed the lamp. And not only that, but it was just as he shouted, 'GAH, I WISH I COULD GET OFF THIS STUPID RIDE. I'M GOING TO BE SICK!'

And that's when Grant disappeared from the gift shop and appeared in front of Sidney Snoop, who thought he must be seeing things.

'Wh-who are YOU?!' he asked, still spinning and spinning round and round.

'I am Grant the Genie and I'm here to grant you your wish!' Grant replied. Then he said his magic wishy word:

'Alaka-blaM-a-bUMWhistle!'

Sidney looked baffled. There was a loud bang, a cloud of smoke and lots of shimmery stars appeared.

As the cloud cleared, Sidney Snoop wasn't on the teacup ride any more.

'Phew,' he said. 'Thank GOODNESS I'm off that awful ride!'

But before he had the chance to take a breath, he started screaming again.

'GENIE, WHAT HAVE YOU DONE? I WANTED TO GET OFF THE RIDE!'

'Well, you are OFF that ride, but we seem to be ON another one!' Grant apologised.

Grant was right – he HAD taken Sidney

off the teacup ride, but now they were ON

the *SUPER DOOPER LOOPY LOOPER* –

the only ride in the world with 100 loop-

da-loops, and they were

only on loop number two.

Sidney Snoop felt
even more sick.
'Genie, GET ME OFF THIS
LOOP-DA-LOOP!'
he shouted angrily.

'You have to say, "I **WISH** you would get me off this loop-da-loop!"' Grant explained.

'Fine! **I WISH** you would get me off this loop-da-loop! **NOW!**' Sidney shouted at Grant.

Another cloud of smoke and more stars appeared, then they vanished to reveal . . . Sidney with his eyes shut tight, sitting on another ride.

'OH NO! What ride am I on **NOW?**' he screamed, seriously close to throwing up. Grant giggled. 'I think you'll be okay on this one.'

Slowly, Sidney opened his eyes and saw that he was sitting on a tiny children's merry-go-round called the **Cutesy-Wutesy Unicorny** ride. He breathed a huge sigh of relief.

'I can't believe you're a real genie,' Sidney said, blinking at Grant. 'A terrible one, but a genie nonetheless! And if I'm not mistaken, I have one wish left!' He grinned.

'Yes, that's right,' Grant replied. 'But please do hurry – I need to get back to my friends.'

'Ah yes – the little girl and her strange dog! Ho ho, oh no, I'm not rushing my last wish! I'm going to be **rich, RICH!**' And, with that, he grabbed Grant, shoved him into the tea-lamp and held his thumb over the spout.

Grant was **TRAPPED!**

CHAPTER 11

WHERE iS GRANT?

'Grant, Grant! **Where are you?**'

Tilly shouted through the park. Since Grant
had disappeared in the gift shop, Tilly and
Teeny had been searching for him, but they
couldn't find him anywhere.

Teeny got down on his hands and knees and started to sniff the ground, then '**WOOF! WOOF!**' he woofed – he had picked up Grant's scent! He raced along, the people in the queues all bewildered at the sight of a small boy on all fours sniffing the floor at such a pace.

It did look rather funny!

Tilly followed behind, looking a bit embarrassed. 'Erm, my brother's dropped his sweets and is trying to find them,' she told everybody, as Teeny continued to sniff out Grant.

Teeny's nose took him around the dodgems, up and down the helter-skelter, past the Dull Duck Lake, and through the funhouse, until – eventually – BUMP! Teeny bumped into a pair of horribly familiar feet. He looked up and there, looking down at him, was Sidney Snoop, holding the tea-lamp. Grant was nowhere to be seen.

Tilly caught up with them and squared up to Sidney.

'Can we have our teapot back, please?' Tilly asked him.

'**No,** you cannot! I know that you know that I know what you know about you-know-who! And I'm taking him to the newspapers and I'm going to make a fortune out of him. **Mwah-ha-ha-ha!'** Sidney cackled, then ran off as

fast as he could, further into the theme park.

Tilly and Teeny gave chase. 'Don't worry, Grant, we'll get you out of there!' Tilly called.

Grant was trying to watch everything that was going on through the crack in the side of his tea-lamp, but it was really difficult . . .

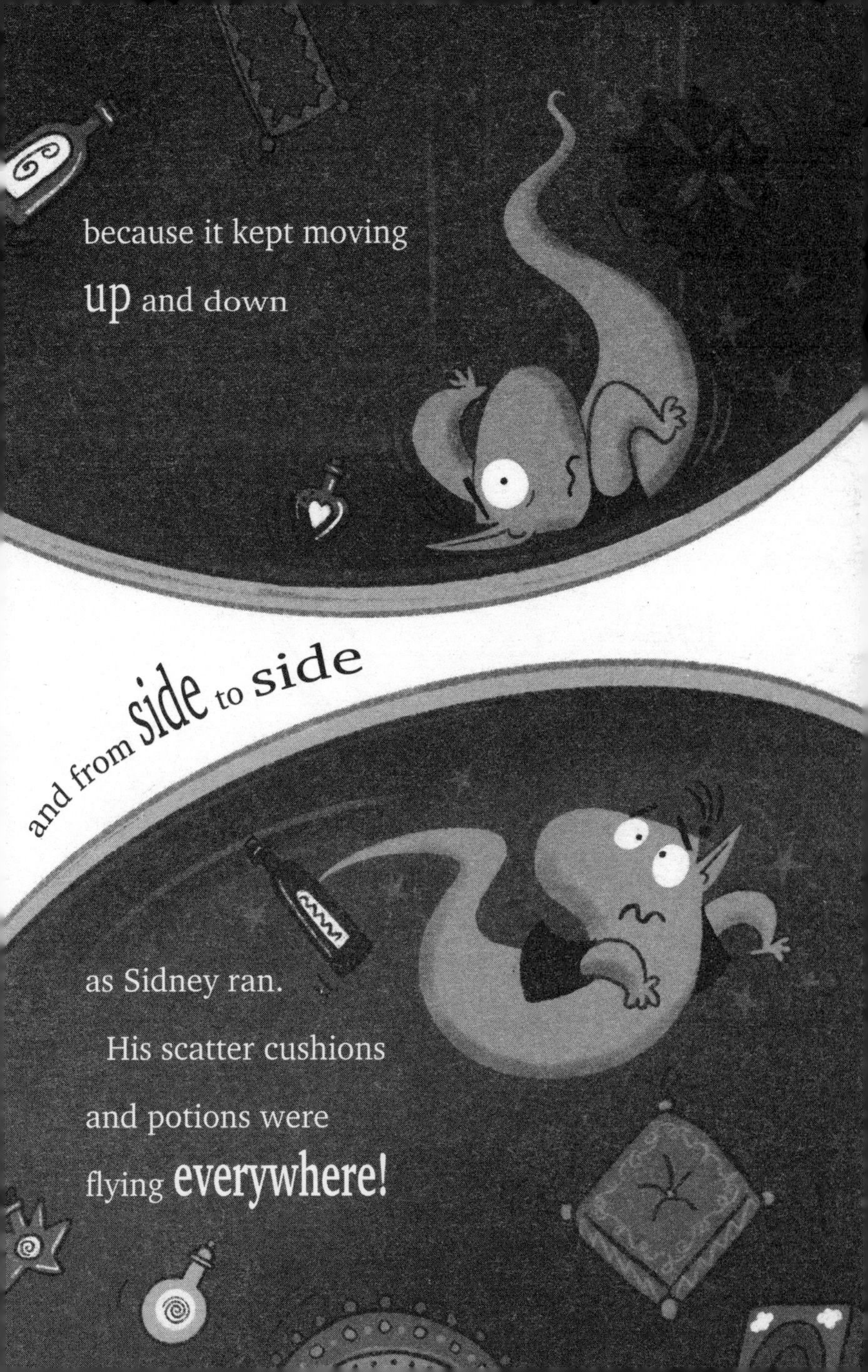

because it kept moving

UP and down

and from **side** to **side**

as Sidney ran.

His scatter cushions
and potions were
flying **everywhere!**

Sidney ran back through the funhouse, past the Dull Duck Lake, up and down the helter-skelter, around the dodgems and into the arcade.

'We've got him cornered,' Tilly said to Teeny, who nodded in agreement.

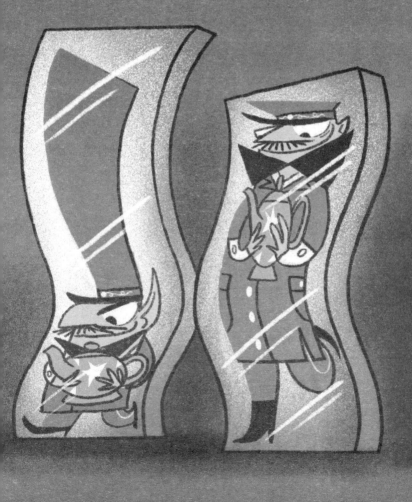

CHAPTER 12

GRAB HiM!

Inside the arcade there were air-hockey tables, football and basketball video games, and mini trampolines. There were lots of over-sized toy prizes, and games machines in all shapes and sizes with bright flashing lights and funny loud sounds. In the centre was the

GIANT GRABBER – a toy-grabbing game

with a huge claw dangling down from the

ceiling.

'Teeny, I have an idea!' Tilly got a crayon

out of her rucksack and drew a quick plan on

the back of the park map.

THE 'SUPER-DUPER
SiDNEY SNOOPER
GRABBER PLAN!

Giant
Grabber →

ARCADE
GAME

Skateboard

②

Beach
Ball

Sick
Slick

Plank

①

Then Tilly went to one of the basketball game machines, put a coin in and quickly beat the high score (a hundred baskets in thirty seconds). She took the string of tickets that she had won and exchanged them for a skateboard and a giant beach ball.

She put the skateboard on the floor near a child who looked like they were about to be sick (they must have just got off the *LOOPY LOOPER* ride), and then Tilly placed a plank of wood over the giant beach ball, all in front of the GIANT GRABBER.

'Right, Teeny, go and sniff out Sidney! When you find him, grab the tea-lamp and run back to me here – go, go, go!'

Teeny saluted Tilly and got back on all fours, sniffing the ground. Sidney smelt of greasy old cheese and fried onions with a hint of gherkin, so it shouldn't take long to find him.

Teeny's nose led him over a table-tennis table, along the bowling lane, across a dancing game, then finally to Sidney, who was heading towards the fire exit!

Teeny barked as loudly as he could and Sidney spun around.

'YOU AGAIN!' Sidney snarled.

'You'll never get your genie back, dog-boy. **Mwah-ha-ha-ha!'** he cackled.

Sidney turned back round but ran straight into a pillar, letting go of the tea-lamp, which flew across the arcade!

Teeny jumped into the air and caught it.

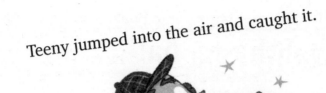

'WAY TO GO, TEENY –
GOOD CATCH!'

Grant shouted as
he flew out of the
spout. He was
finally free!

Teeny and Grant blew raspberries at Sidney and rushed off.

Sidney, dazed, shook his head and ran after them. 'Bring back my genie!' he shouted as he gave chase.

Teeny and Grant skidded to a halt next to Tilly in the centre of the arcade.

Sidney was fast approaching, so the next part of Tilly's plan went into action. She held out

the tea-lamp towards Sidney, who went to grab it JUST as the ill-looking child vomited right in front of him. Sidney SKIDDED through the lumpy yellow puddle and landed

on the skateboard. The skateboard whizzed forwards and smacked into an arcade game, CATAPULTING Sidney through the air until he landed on the bouncy ball see-saw.

'NOW!' Tilly shouted as she, Teeny and Grant all jumped on to the other end of the see-saw, and Sidney flew UP AND OVER into the pile of toys inside the GIANT GRABBER.

BOING!

Tilly put a coin in the slot and used the joystick to move the ginormous claw over Sidney before hitting the red button. The giant claw whirred into action and moved along then stopped. Tilly hit the next button and the claw moved down towards Sidney's bottom.

'NOOOO!' he screamed as it grabbed him and raised him into the air.

Tilly unplugged the machine. Sidney was stuck.

He waggled his legs and hands. The entire arcade looked up and laughed at Sidney as he shouted, 'GET ME DOWN! I WANT MY GENIE BACK!'

'Come on, guys – let's get to that **CRAZY CLOUD COASTER!**' Tilly said to Teeny and Grant as she put the tea-lamp safely back in her backpack.

CHAPTER 13

THE CRAZY CLOUD COASTER

'There it is!' Tilly shouted as they turned a

corner and saw the huge sign for the **CRAZY**

CLOUD COASTER.

'Grant, we **made** it! . . . Grant? Where have

you gone **NOW?**' Tilly said, frustrated.

'**WOOF!**' woofed Teeny, pointing to the **MAGIC FLYING CARPET** ride next door.

Grant was floating towards it.

'Ooh, it's been ages since I've been on a magic carpet ride!' he said, looking longingly at the big purple-and-gold flying carpet in front of him.

'Oh no you don't, Grant! We can't risk you getting captured again!' replied Tilly, as she and Teeny caught up with him. 'Come on, we've got to get you home!'

Grant sighed and sat on Tilly's shoulder.

'You're right, of course, Tilly – onward to the **CRAZY CLOUD COASTER!**'

CHAPTER 14

ACTUALLY
THE
CRAZY
CLOUD COASTER

WAIT TIME FROM THIS POINT 90 MINUTES

Tilly, Teeny and Grant joined the back of the long queue. They looked up at the sign above them that said:

WAIT TIME FROM THIS POINT 90 MINUTES.

'Ninety minutes?' said Tilly desperately. 'We

can't wait that long! Urgh, I wish we were at the front of the queue— OOPS!' Tilly put her hand over her mouth as she realised what she had just said.

'Your wish is my command, Tilly,' said Grant.

'Alaka-blam-a-bumwhistle!'

And in a cloud of turquoise smoke, they WERE at the front of the queue.

But it was the queue for the ladies' toilets.

'Oh, Grant!' Tilly giggled.

'Alaka-blam-a-bumwhistle!'

. . . and in another cloud of smoke and

stars, they reappeared at the front of the CRAZY CLOUD COASTER queue!

'Yikes! I did it!' Grant said, smiling with glee.

'Two, is it?' the woman working on the ride asked them.

'Yes, please,' Tilly replied. 'This is it, guys!' she said excitedly to Teeny and Grant, who was sitting on her shoulder.

The woman led them to the very front of the roller coaster and put the safety harnesses over Tilly and Teeny's heads. Teeny was panting with excitement.

Grant popped into his tea-lamp and came back wearing his crash helmet, goggles and cape.

'What's the cape for, Grant? Is it magical?
Does it help you fly better? Tilly asked.

'**No,** I just like the **colour,**' Grant said,
and he giggled.

'Oh, Grant, I'm really going to **miss** you,' Tilly said with a tear in her eye.

'And I am really going to miss you and Teeny, too,' he replied with a lump in his throat.

'But it's so exciting that you will soon be back home with your dad and sister. Remember the plan?'

'Yes,' said Grant. 'As soon as we get to the top of the highest part of the roller coaster, I jump on to the nearest cloud and keep going until I reach WISHALUZIA!'

CHAPTER 15

JUMP!

'Get ready for the tallest, fastest, craziest, cloudiest ride of your life!' the woman announced over the loudspeaker.

'In three,

two,

ONE –

BLAST OFF!'

The rocket-shaped roller coaster zoomed forwards!

Tilly held on for dear life.

Teeny's hat flew straight off, and his ears and tongue were flapping around like mad.

Grant was tucked in under Tilly's safety harness and was holding on tight. 'Woohooooo! This is AMAZING!' shouted Grant as they sped around the first bend and into the next, picking up even more speed as they went through a corkscrew-like section.

Then the ride slowed down slightly and they went through a tunnel. It was dark at first, but then lots of bright lights lit up the space. There were moving models of clouds, rainbows, rockets, stars and winged creatures.

Grant gasped. 'Wow! This is beautiful!' he said.

The ride then suddenly zoomed forwards again even faster than before and started to go up a very, very, VERY steep hill.

'Grant, this is it – the tallest bit of the ride!' Tilly shouted.

'WOOOOOOF!' woofed Teeny.

As they got higher and higher, the ride raced past birds and even an aeroplane, it was getting SO high.

'Grant, get ready to jump! I can see the top of the ride . . . and LOOK!' Tilly pointed.

There in the distance, sitting on a huge white cloud, was a beautiful, shining city in all the colours of the rainbow, surrounded by shimmering stars.

'It's my home!' Grant replied with a tear in his eye. 'It's WISHALUZIA!'

'It's time, Grant – you must go!' Tilly told him.

Grant went to jump from the roller coaster . . .

. . . but he couldn't – his cape was caught under the safety harness. **He was stuck!**

Tilly and Teeny tried to help, but it was **too** late! Grant looked up at WISHALUZIA and reached towards it, but just then the ride plummeted downwards, taking Grant with it.

'**Oh no,** Grant, you didn't make it!' Tilly cried as they zoomed down for miles, back through the clouds. After some more twists and turns, they were back at the beginning of the ride. It stopped with a jerk.

'Don't worry, Tilly,' he said. 'We can just go round again!'

'Oh yes,' said Tilly. 'Good thinking!' and she giggled.

But just then a message came over the loudspeaker: 'Ladies and gentlemen, boys and girls, we are sorry to announce that, due to a technical fault, the **CRAZY CLOUD COASTER** is now CLOSED for repair.'

'NOOOO!' Tilly cried.

'Oh, 'eck!' said Grant.

'woof!' Teeny woofed sadly, as they got off the ride and walked back to the entrance.

CHAPTER 16

WELL, WELL, WELL!

Tilly bought them all a snack and a drink to try and cheer themselves up. They sat down on the side of a funny old well that had a sign next to it saying: **THE WISHING WELL.**

'Oh, Grant, this is a disaster!' Tilly said, giving him a hug. 'We'll have to come back another day, I guess, but it will be tricky sneaking out again without Mum knowing,' she said. 'We might have to wait quite a while until we can try again. I'm so sorry, Grant. I guess we can turn Teeny back to normal now, though.'

Grant nodded, clicked his fingers and, just as Teeny was about to tuck into his hot dog, there was a loud **BANG**, a cloud of smoke . . . and boy-Teeny was dog-Teeny again.

'WOW, first time, Grant! **Well done!**'
Tilly said.

Teeny licked Grant and Tilly, then ate his
hot dog in one big gulp.

'It's all this cape's fault. I shouldn't have put
the stupid thing on,' said Grant, taking it off.
'How I wish I was back home in Genie World.'
He crumpled up the cape and threw it into
the wishing well.

They began to walk away, but suddenly they
heard a strange, magical sound. They turned
around and saw stars sparkling and twinkling
around the wishing well.

'What's happening, Grant?' Tilly asked.
'No idea!' he replied.

They looked down into the well and saw that the water was now all the colours of the rainbow, swirling round and round like an amazing magical washing machine.

Suddenly, without warning, a turquoise hand appeared from the whirlpool, grabbed Grant and pulled him into a portal.

'*HELP!*'

Grant screamed.

'Grant, **noooooo!**' called Tilly as she tried to grab his hand, but it was too late – Grant had vanished!

Just then Sidney Snoop appeared with a big net, running towards Tilly and Teeny. **'I KNEW YOU WERE A DOG!** Now I've **GOTCHA!'** he shouted as he swung the net towards Teeny.

But Teeny was fast and he jumped into the well.

'**Teeny, no!**' cried Tilly, but Teeny had vanished too!

'**Give me back my genie!**' Sidney shouted at Tilly as he moved closer towards her.

Tilly was right on the edge of the wishing

well and, as Sidney Snoop raised his net, she

fell backwards into the well and disappeared.

'Ha! Now I've got you all!' Sidney cried, and he laughed as he walked up to the wishing well and looked inside, expecting to find Tilly, Teeny and the genie. But instead, there was just some water and his own reflection . . .

CHAPTER 17

WHERE HAVE THEY GONE?

'WOOOOOOAAAAH!' Grant shouted.

He was zooming through a colourful,

sparkly magic tunnel at great speed.

Teeny and Tilly were following behind,

flying past stars and beautiful swirly shapes.

Up ahead, Grant could see a very bright shimmering light and, as he whooshed towards it, he closed his eyes. Then Grant flew out of a swirling portal that looked like the one in the wishing well and landed with a soft bounce on a fluffy white cloud!

Teeny then zoomed out of the portal, closely followed by Tilly, bouncing off the cloud and landing in a heap next to Grant.

Then a shadow loomed towards them.

And the shadow spoke . . .

'Grant? . . . is that **YOU?**'

Grant recognised that voice!

He looked up and there, smiling at him, was a very familiar face.

Not only had Genie, Teeny and Tilly found their way to WISHALUZIA, they had also found Grant's sister!

'**Oh,** Grant, h0W we have **missed you!**' she said, sweeping him up in her arms and giving him a huge squeeze.

'Oh, Greta, it's **so good** to see you!'
said Grant, beaming, and they did a funny
greeting, sticking their tongues out at each
other, waggling their hands, touching elbows
then flying round each other in a circle.

'But **who are** these creatures?' Greta asked,
looking at Tilly and Teeny.

'These are my friends from Earth,' Grant replied with a smile. 'Tilly and Teeny, meet Greta, my sister.'

'Hello, I'm Tilly,' Tilly said, standing up and shaking Greta's hand.

'**woof woof!**' Teeny woofed, licking Greta's face.

Greta giggled then suddenly looked serious.

'We'd better get back home,' she said. 'It's getting late and Dad will be wondering where I've got to. He'll be over the moon to see you, Grant!'

'This is **so exciting!**' said Tilly. 'I can't believe we are in Genie World!'

So Grant, Tilly and Teeny followed Greta

through the sparkly, cloudy landscape of WISHALUZIA until they reached what looked like a neighbourhood of giant magical lamps – of all shapes, colours and sizes.

One particular lamp stood out from all the others because it looked really funny. It had three wonky spouts, two handles and some oddly shaped windows.

'Ah, home sweet home!' sighed Grant.

Tilly giggled. 'I had a feeling this might be where you live,' she said.

'Here we go, guys!' Greta said as she wiggled her nose, and the four of them disappeared in a cloud of pink smoke.

CHAPTER 18

BOO!

With a flash of sparkly stars, they all
reappeared inside the funny lamp.

'**Wow,** this is amazing!' Tilly said,
gazing around at all the weird and wonderful
trinkets, furniture, lanterns and decorations.

'Sshhh,' whispered Greta. 'Let's really surprise Dad and jump out at him!'

Grant giggled. 'Oh, Greta, you are a one! Okay, let's all hide.'

Tilly hid inside a big, fancy-looking vase and Teeny hid underneath a table. Grant disappeared behind a curtain and Greta flew behind a book on one of the shelves.

Then they waited. And they waited. And they waited some more.

'Daaaaad!' Greta eventually shouted.

'What?' Dad shouted back.

'I'm home!' Greta replied.

'Oh, good. HELLO,' shouted Dad.

'Well, are you coming down to see me?'

Greta shouted back.

'I'm in the loo! I'll be down in a minute,' Dad shouted back again.

They all giggled and waited. And they waited a bit longer.

Then they heard the loo flush and a door close. Grant's dad floated down the stairs and they all jumped out from their hiding places and shouted:

'BOO!'

'Oh, my CRAZY CARPETS!' Dad shouted

excitedly. 'What in WISHALUZIA...?

Grant! It's you! I was worried I'd never

see you again. Oh, my boy – it's so

WONDERFUL to have you back!'

and he rushed up to Grant and gave him a

massive long hug.

'Oh, Dad, I'm so glad to see you! I really

missed you. And these are my fabulous

friends from Earth –

Tilly and Teeny!'

'It's a pleasure

to welcome

you both to

WISHALUZIA,' said Grant's dad. 'You must stay and have some tea!' He beamed.

'Oh, YES, please, we would LOVE to!' replied Tilly, clapping her hands together.

But just then, an odd-looking clock made a funny chiming sound. It chimed six times.

'Oh, **Teeny!** It's six o'clock!' cried Tilly. 'We have to go. Mum will be wondering where we are. But what are we going to do? I've run out of Grant's wishes!' Tilly panicked.

'Don't worry,' Greta said soothingly. 'Dad and I owe you a big wish for helping to bring Grant back to us!'

'That's right,' Dad said with a nod. 'It's the least we can do.'

CHAPTER 19

A GOODBYE GIFT

'Oh, Tilly, so it really is goodbye this time,'
Grant said, hugging her and Teeny. 'Thank you
so much for everything you've done for me.'

'What an adventure we have had together!'
Tilly said. 'It's been amazing, Grant, thank

you, and I'm so glad you made it back home to your fabulous family at last.'

'**WAIT – I have an idea!**' Grant shouted.

He flew up to his room and reappeared with a small, odd-shaped mirror.

'This is a magic mirror that belonged to my grandma,' he said, handing the mirror to her. 'If you ever need us, Tilly, look into it and say "WISHALUZIA!" three times.

It will bring me to you.'

Tilly placed it in her pocket and hugged Grant once more.

'Thank you so much, Grant,' she said with a tear in her eye.

'It's time to make your wish, Tilly,' Greta said.

Tilly nodded and picked up Teeny.

'I wish to be back home,' she said, waving goodbye to everyone.

Greta wiggled her nose and said her magic wishy word:

'Poodle~parp~ a~pipsqueak!'

Then a cloud of pink smoke appeared

and . . . oh!

. . . Tilly and Teeny hadn't gone home. They'd been turned into garden GNOMES! 'Whoops!' they all giggled.

'Let me try,' said Dad, and he wiggled his pointy ears and said his magic wishy word:

Jim-a-jam-a-jumplebumps!'

There was a cloud of green smoke this time and . . . oh!

. . . Tilly and Teeny still weren't home. This time they were covered in FOAM.

Teeny licked it all off.

Then Greta had an idea. 'I know, let's all try together!' she exclaimed.

The three genies nodded, then all held hands.

'I wish to be back home!' Tilly said again.

The genies all wiggled their noses and ears and said their magic wishy words.

There was a loud BANG and a big cloud of pink, turquoise and green smoke.

The genie family slowly opened their eyes . . . and Tilly and Teeny were gone.

CHAPTER 20
BACK
HOME

Tilly and Teeny also opened their eyes and, to their amazement, they were sitting in their kitchen. And just in time, too, because here was Mum coming out of the study, having finished a phone call.

'**Hello, my lovelies!** Did you have a nice day?' she asked.

'It was okay, thanks,' Tilly replied, winking at Teeny.

'Wonderful! You must tell me all about it over dinner,' said Mum as she started to chop some tomatoes.

'I'll just pop upstairs and wash my hands, Mum,' Tilly said. 'I won't be a minute.'

Tilly ran to her bedroom, closely followed by Teeny, and they both sat on her bed.

Tilly felt in her pocket, took out the magic mirror, looked into it and smiled at her reflection. She felt comforted that she would see Grant again one day.

'Come on – dinner's ready, guys!' Mum called up the stairs.

'Coming, Mum!' Tilly called back, and she put the mirror on her bedside table.

HOW TO DRAW GENIE'S TEA-LAMP

1 Start by drawing a circle.

2 Draw two curved lines to create the handle.

3 Then draw more curvy lines to make the spout.

Add a small circle at the top and a curved line to make the lid.

5

Then draw the base on the bottom of the lamp.

6

Finally, add stars for decoration and use a yellow crayon to colour it in.

STEVEN LENTON is a multi-award-winning illustrator, originally from Cheshire, now working from his studios in Brighton and London with his French bulldog, Big-Eared Bob!

He has illustrated many children's books, including *Head Kid* and *Future Friend* by David Baddiel, *The Hundred and One Dalmatians* adapted by Peter Bently, the Shifty McGifty and Slippery Sam series by Tracey Corderoy, Frank Cottrell-Boyce's fiction titles and Steven Butler's Sainsbury's Prize-winning The Nothing to See Here Hotel series.

He has illustrated two World Book Day titles and regularly appears at literary festivals, live events and schools across the UK.

Steven has his own Draw-Along-A-Lenton YouTube channel, showing you how to draw a range of his characters, and he was in the Top 20 Bookseller Bestselling Illustrator Chart 2019.

The Genie and Teeny series is Steven's first foray into children's fiction and he really hopes you are enjoying Grant and Teeny's adventures!

Find out more about Steven and his work at stevenlenton.com.